Big Monster is Running Away

Jeanne Willis
Illustrated by Deborah Jones

"I am running away," said Big Monster.

"Why are you running away?" said Dog.

"Are you running away from home?" said Cat.

"Are you running away from school?" said Rabbit.

"No," said Big Monster.
"I am running away from . . .